Trip To The Building

Kamden

Langston

Trip To The Building

Trip To The Building

1st Trip To The Building

LCCN 2020911498

Site Tools

Monkey Wrench

Oil Can

Hammer

Screwdrivers

On the 1st day of each month, Mr. Morris's plan was the same. He would put on his clothes, boots, and tools. But on this day, he noticed something a little strange. He could see from across the room that his tools were rearranged.

Mr. Morris went to look for the twins in their room. There stood Langston in front of the mirror. Langston was wearing his tool belt, and Kamden's demeanor had changed.

Kamden was pacing around the room, calling himself "Mr. Morris."

Mr. Morris smiled and said, "One day, all that you see will be yours. Get your jackets. We are going for a ride. It is time for your first property tour."

"Where are we going?" asked the boys. Mr. Morris replied, "We are going to the building to do some chores, and for you to see what will soon be yours."

A voice on the other side of the door said, "Tell him I don't have his money and to return another day."
"Fair enough," says Mr. Morris, "I will catch him before he gets away, but most importantly enjoy your day."

The crew dashed up the stairs and went to the next door.
Three knocks on the door and Mr. Morris said, "Today is
the day that I collect your pay, no ifs, ands, or buts.
I only want to hear you say okay."

The tenant replied, "I have your rent, but this annoying **drip, drip, drip** is really not fair. Please stop the drip with one of your trusty repairs."

Mr. Morris said, "Don't worry, just stop and think. Bring my tools and place them next to the sink."

"Dad," said Kamden "What do you need? I'm ready to listen and take heed." "Okay," said Mr. Morris. "Put on your gloves before you proceed. Now hand me the tool that you think I will need."

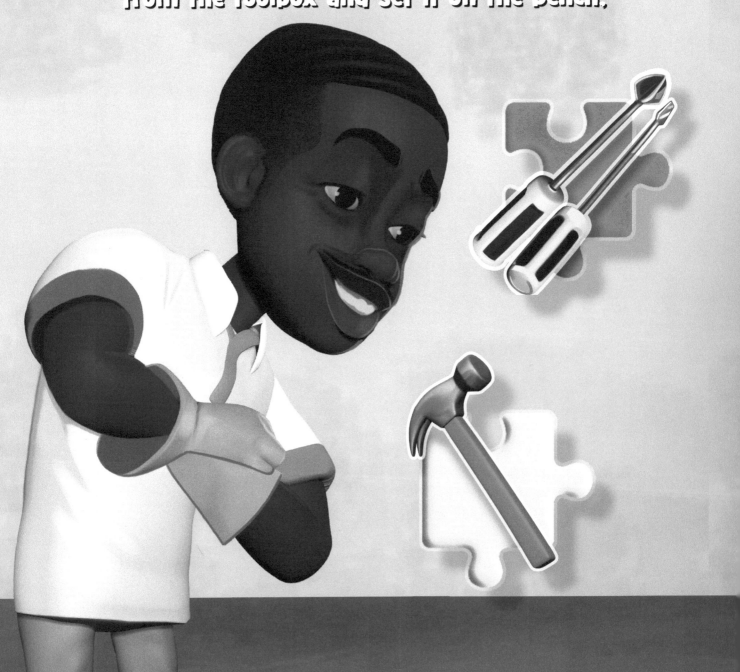

"I need the monkey wrench," Mr. Morris said. "Grab it from the toolbox and set it on the bench."

"Where's the monkey and what's a wrench?" asked Kamden.

Mr. Morris replied, "The wrench is silver and is used to twist and turn. Pay attention so you can learn."

"But, I don't know which way to turn the wrench," said Kamden.

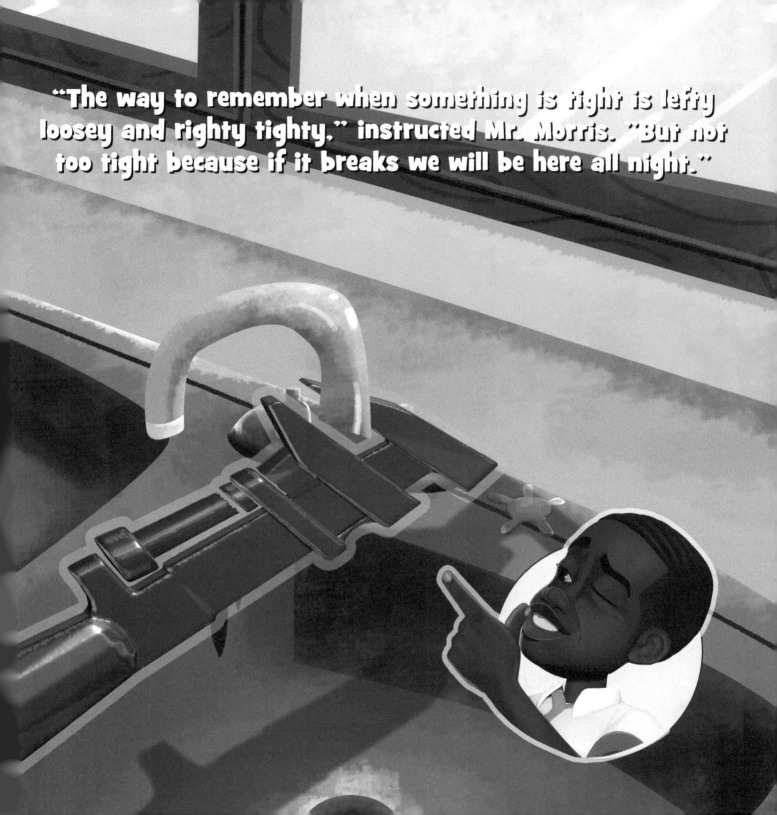

"The way to remember when something is tight is lefty loosey and righty tighty," instructed Mr. Morris. "But not too tight because if it breaks we will be here all night."

After completing the repair, they dashed up the stairs to the next tenant's door. Three knocks on the door, and they yelled out together, "Today is the day that I collect your pay. No ifs, ands, or buts.
"I only want to hear you say okay."

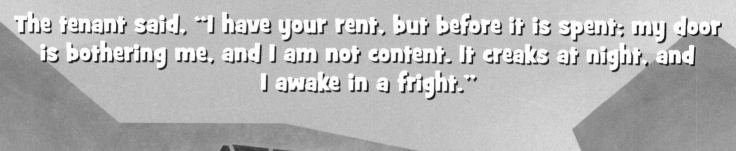

The tenant said, "I have your rent, but before it is spent; my door is bothering me, and I am not content. It creaks at night, and I awake in a fright."

"Dad," Langston asked. "What tool do you need? I am ready to learn this deed."

The repair is done, no worries anymore, and
they dash up the stairs to the final door.

Mr. Morris replied, "I like your eagerness, little man, grab the oil that's in the can."

Three knocks on the door and you heard them say. "Today is the day that I collect your pay. No ifs, ands, or buts. I only want to hear you say okay."

"Dad, what tool do we use?"
Langston asked.

"A hammer and nails will work very well.
Just bang, bang, bang until you
remove that swell."

"Keep striking and striking it
until you no longer see the swell," said Mr. Morris.

The repair is complete, no worries anymore. They dashed up the stairs but stopped because the banister had fallen on the floor.

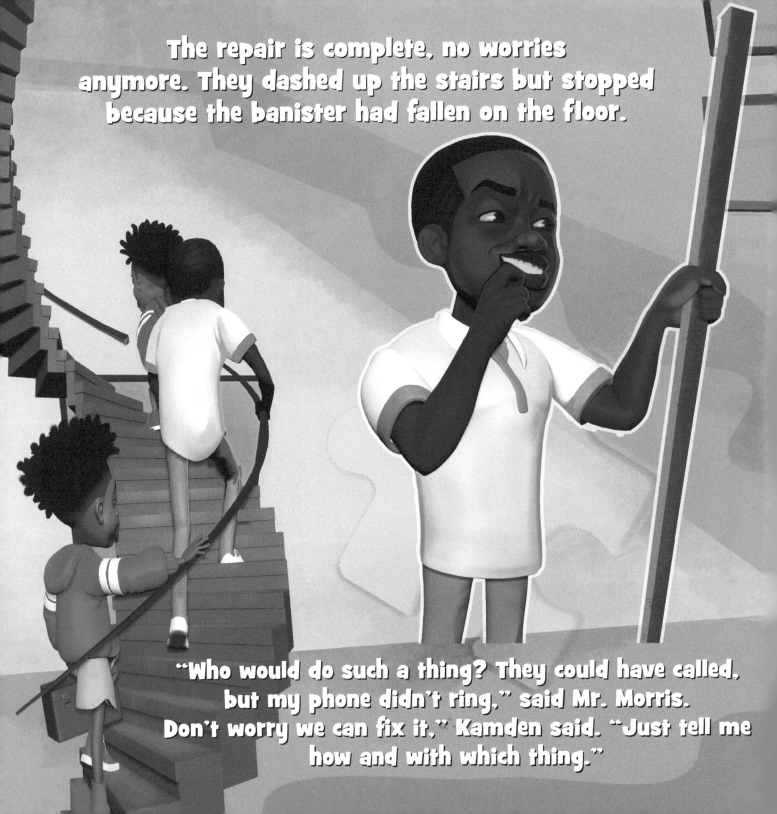

"Who would do such a thing? They could have called, but my phone didn't ring," said Mr. Morris. Don't worry we can fix it," Kamden said. "Just tell me how and with which thing."

"That 'thing' would be a screwdriver and grab three long screws. The screws will be at the bottom of the toolbox, along with the rest of the tools," Mr. Morris said.

"Daddy, what's a screwdriver?" Kamden asked.

Mr. Morris explained, "The screwdriver is long with an X" shaped tip." It matches the screw head, and has the yellow rubber grip,"

The twins asked "What about the guy who told us to wait?" Mr. Morris said "There's always tomorrow. No need to debate. But I did leave a 5-day notice with his mate."

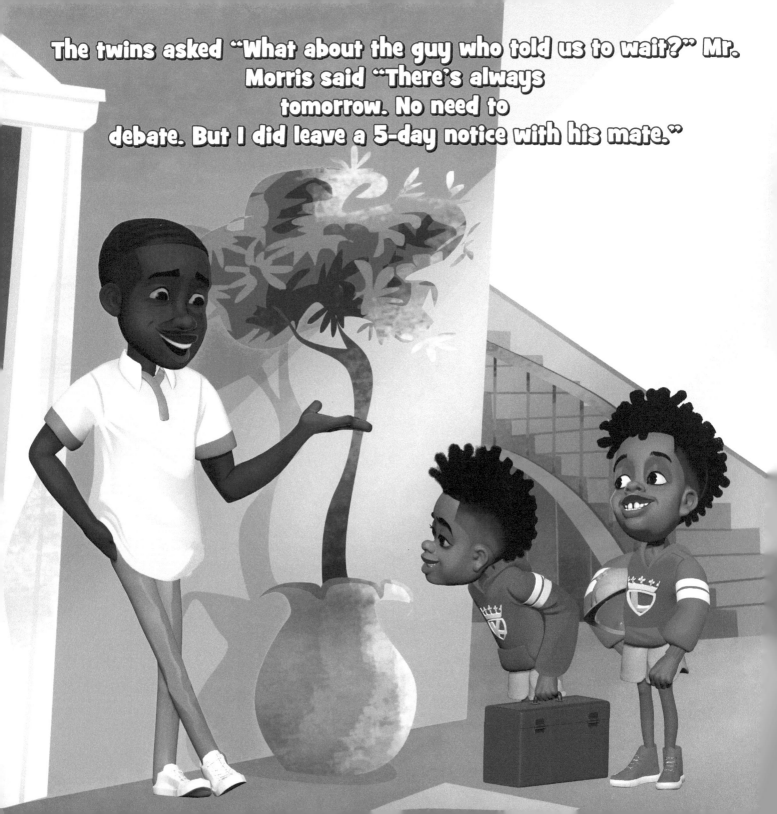

"I had fun today, especially when we collected the pay." Kamden exclaimed. "I think our name should be KLM." Langston protested, "I'm the oldest, Kamden, so I get the last say. The name will be LKM, let's keep that straight."

Hammer

Monkey Wrench

Screwdrivers

Oil Can

About the Author:

James Morris Jr. was born and raised in Chicago, Illinois. He is an economist for the federal government, an investor, and a real estate coach for new investors interested in property ownership. James earned a Bachelors of Science degree in Economics from the University of Illinois at Urbana-Champaign. He is the father of three intelligent children; their names are Langston, Kamden, and Kerrington (daughter). Knowing the importance of educating his children about property ownership, investing, financial literacy, and generational wealth, he began writing a series of children books that will reflect children of color and the importance of building generational wealth. James hopes that his books inspire parents to understand the importance of financial literacy
for themselves and their children.

facebook.com @MorrisChildrenBooks

 Email: Admin@morrischildrenbooks.com

 www.morrischildrenbooks.com

The Illustrator:

Tyrus Goshay is an award-winning digital illustrator and 3D artist with over 18 years of experience. He serves as a college professor, teaching both game design, and illustration in his off time. Tyrus has a bachelor's in Computer Animation and Multimedia and a master's degree in Teaching With Technology (MALT). He has contributed to several award-winning projects in the world of Toy design and has been recognized for his achievements in academia as well. He also has tutorials in illustration and digital sculpting available on the web.
Visit his bookstore, and see other books that he has illustrated.

www.facebook.com/Tgosketch

Email: Tgosketch@gmail.com

Instagram: Tgosketch

www.tgosketch.com

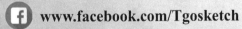
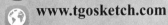

CPSIA information can be obtained
at www.ICGtesting.com
Printed in the USA
LVHW071908051120
670843LV00002B/60